WHAT A TREE IT WILL BE!™

STORY BY L. S. V. BAKER

PICTURES & ILLUSTRATIONS BY M. E. B. STOTTMANN

Published by

"What A Tree It Will Be!"

For information, address Baxter's Corner, P.O. Box 223, Harrods Creek, KY 40027.
www.BaxtersCorner.com

Library of Congress Control Number: 2012921980

ISBN 978-1-938647-04-8

First Printing, November 2012
V2.0

Dedicated to my parents, Wayne and Margaret, for encouraging me to explore my creative abilities even when I "clumped" the icicles on our family Christmas Tree.

In Mr. McBoom's class
the kids were giddy with glee.
They were imagining the biggest, the brightest,
the sparkliest tree.

Mr. McBoom told his class,
"I think you will find
this special tree I have found
is what you had in mind."

The kids took one look.
They couldn't believe
that this bundle of branches
was the class Christmas tree.

Mr. McBoom told the kids,
"This is a most extraordinary tree.
In its branches hides beauty
that is now hard to see.

"Once each of you adds
your special touch to the tree,
it will amaze and astound you.
What a tree it will be!"

Ally spoke up.
"I can help this tree stand
and give it the start that it needs
so that it will look grand."

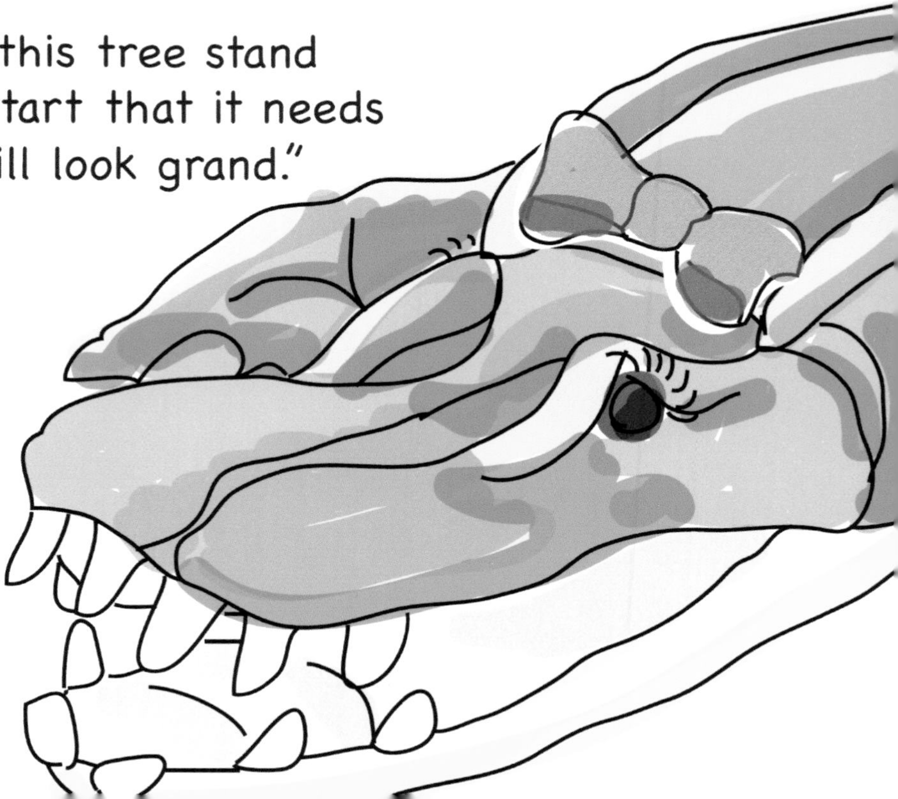

Oakley looked at the tree.
The branches were thin on one side.
Using all of his arms,
he spread the branches out wide.

Tajo thought the tree was too dark.
It needed some light.
He crawled deep inside with some bulbs
to make the tree bright.

Olivia knew that some ornaments
would fill the blank spaces.
She swung branch-to-branch hanging balls
in the very best places.

Fred grabbed some icicles.
Then with a hop,
he decked the tree with sparkling silver
from bottom to top.

Ellema thought, "Every tree needs
a light dusting of snow."
She covered all the tree's branches
with one single blow.

Gerome saw a bare spot
at the tip top of the tree.
He placed a shining gold star there
for everyone to see.

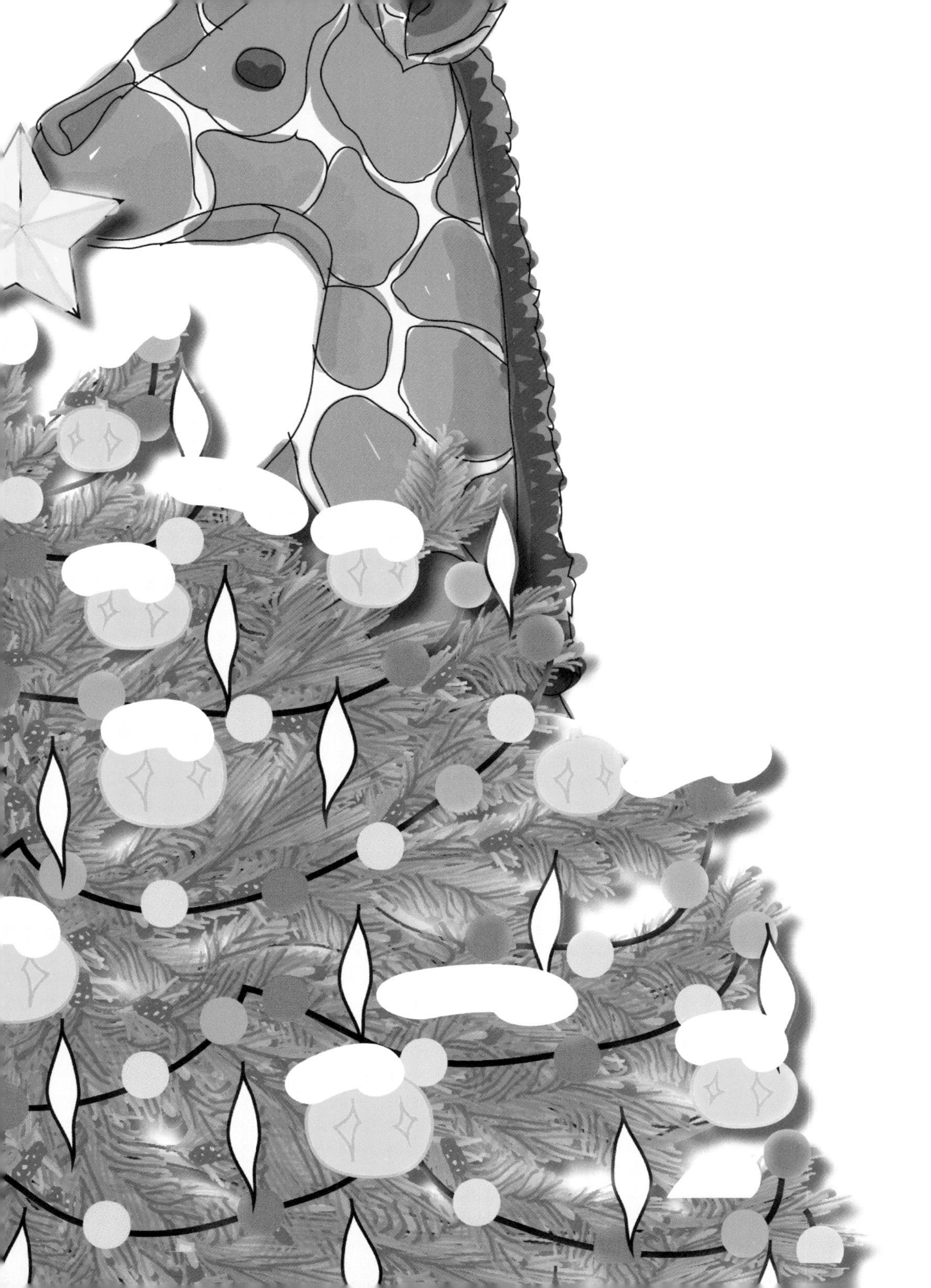

They all gathered around
the freshly trimmed tree.
It was more beautiful than Mr. McBoom
had said it would be!

The lights shone. The star twinkled.
It was big! It was bright!
The tree glittered and sparkled.
It was a wonderful sight.

Mr. McBoom said, "This tree is perfect.
And do you know the reason?
You each gave your best, and
that's the best gift of the season."

The End.

Books - Puppets - Art

Building Character Is Child's Play™

Baxter's Corner provides a "Beyond the Story Book" experience using the story as the foundation that helps teach life's lessons and build character around social skills and fundamental values.

More than just a story, children are engaged through discussion questions and activities included in the books and online at www.BaxtersCorner.com. These activities extend and enrich a child's understanding of the differences and perspectives of others as they develop problem-solving skills and learn how to work together.

Our engaging animal characters wrestle with the same situations and choices that children face. Children will laugh at the predicaments of their new furry friends and find comfort in knowing others face the same challenges.

Along with innovative puppets and vibrant wall art, Baxter's Corner creates a rich environment for children to expand their understanding through play.

Beyond the Storybook

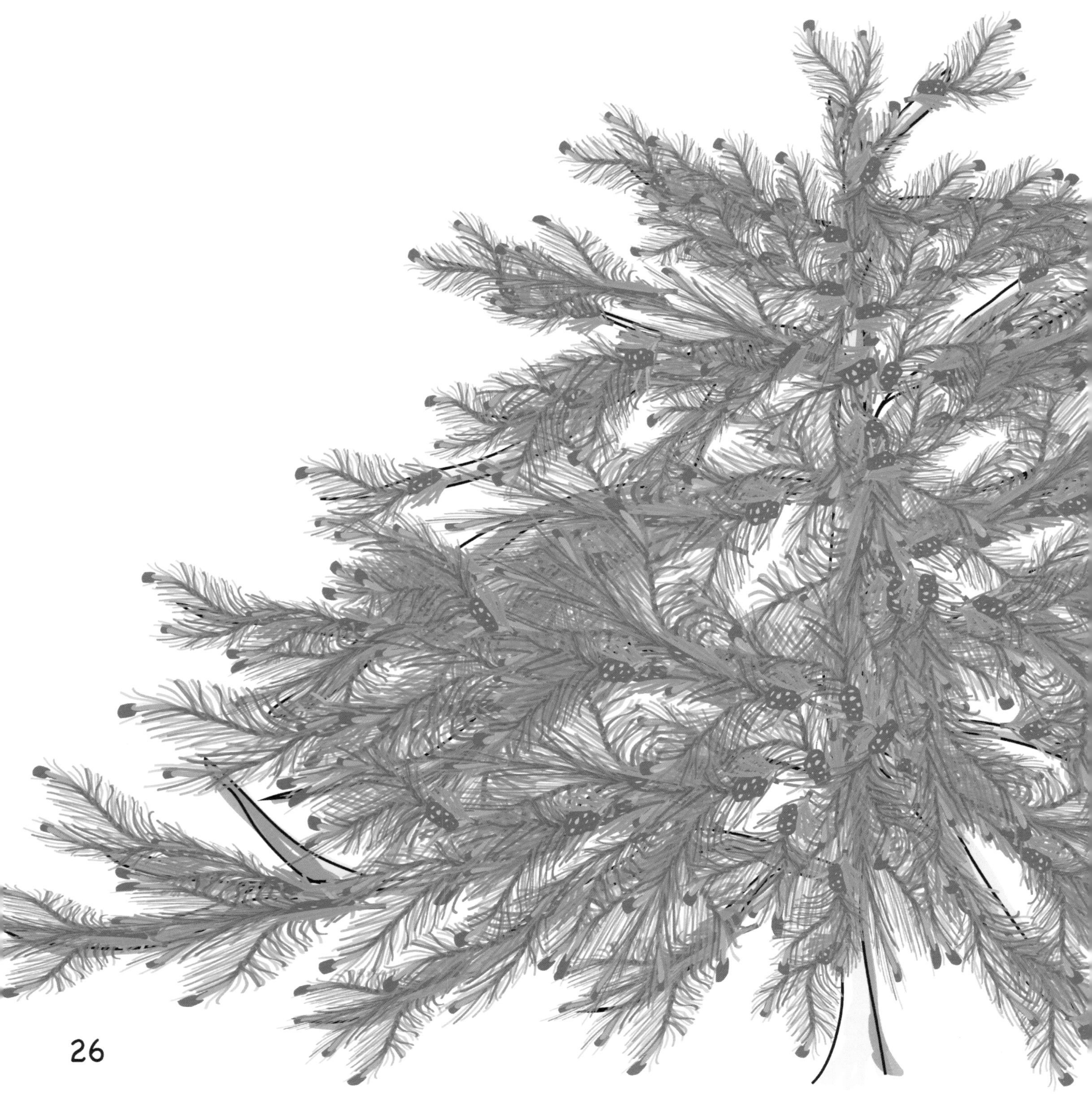

Fun facts about Christmas trees

- Even before the first Christmas, evergreen trees were used by people in ancient history during the long, dark days of winter as a reminder that spring would return, bringing more hours of sunlight to grow plants for food.
- Bringing decorated trees indoors to celebrate Christmas began in Germany in the 16th century.
- The first records of Christmas trees in America date back to the early 1800s. By the 1870s, Christmas trees had become common in America.
- Originally, Christmas trees were decorated with candles, nuts, berries and other types of food.
- Glass ornaments began to be used as decorations on American trees in the late 1800s.
- When electricity arrived, candles on trees were replaced by Christmas lights.
- Franklin Pierce, the 14th president, began the tradition of having an official tree in the White House.
- 34 to 36 million Christmas trees are harvested for sale each year.
- More than 77 million Christmas trees are planted each year. It takes six to eight years for a Christmas tree to mature.
- Christmas trees are grown in all 50 states, including Hawaii and Alaska.

Share the spirit of Christmas

At Christmas, things just seem more fun. We hear Christmas music everywhere we go. We are surrounded by decorations, sparkling lights, and beautiful Christmas trees. We bake cookies, wrap presents, and attend parties. Most importantly, we spend time with our family and friends.

Because of the effort of many people in your life - at home, at school, at church, in the neighborhood - there are decorations to enjoy, gifts to be unwrapped, and special events to attend.

Part of the fun is sharing the spirit of Christmas. So, become an elf for the season!

An elf's duties include being helpful and cheerful. Here are some ways you can spread Christmas cheer:

1. Form an elf patrol.

2. Be an elf volunteer.

3. Become an elf detective.

4. Share elf enthusiasm.

Elf patrol

Watch for ways to be helpful.

- Offer to help carry shopping bags.
- Offer to help put stamps on envelopes for family Christmas cards.
- Hold doors open for others when entering or leaving a building.
- Offer to help with Christmas baking projects, such gathering utensils and decorating cookies.
- Offer to help wrap presents.
- If it snows where you live, offer to help clear snow from your vehicle or shovel the walkway for a neighbor.

Elf volunteer

One of the best gifts you can give is your time. Take time during the Christmas season to participate in volunteer activities to help other people.

Visit with residents of a retirement home, who may not have friends who visit them. You can pass out homemade Christmas cards or sing Christmas carols. Ask your Mom, Dad or caregiver to contact a local retirement home for details on visitor policies and available times.

Help the less fortunate. Most communities have food drives or gift collection centers to gather food, clothing and toys for people who may be homeless, sick or have no money for food. Check with your teacher at school and your Sunday school teacher to learn of opportunities in your neighborhood.

Elf detective

Part of the fun of Christmas is bringing joy to others. Sometimes we are so busy with our own celebrations, that we do not realize there are some people who may be lonely or forgotten at Christmas.

Detectives are people who solve mysteries by looking carefully at clues other people miss. An **Elf Detective** is someone who is careful to look for people who may be alone or who often go overlooked, including:

- an elderly neighbor
- school cafeteria workers
- your bus driver
- the custodian at school

Your mission is to identify people during the Christmas season who are lonely or left out, and make an extra effort to be kind to them and be sure to include them in Christmas activities such as making decorations or sharing Christmas cookies!

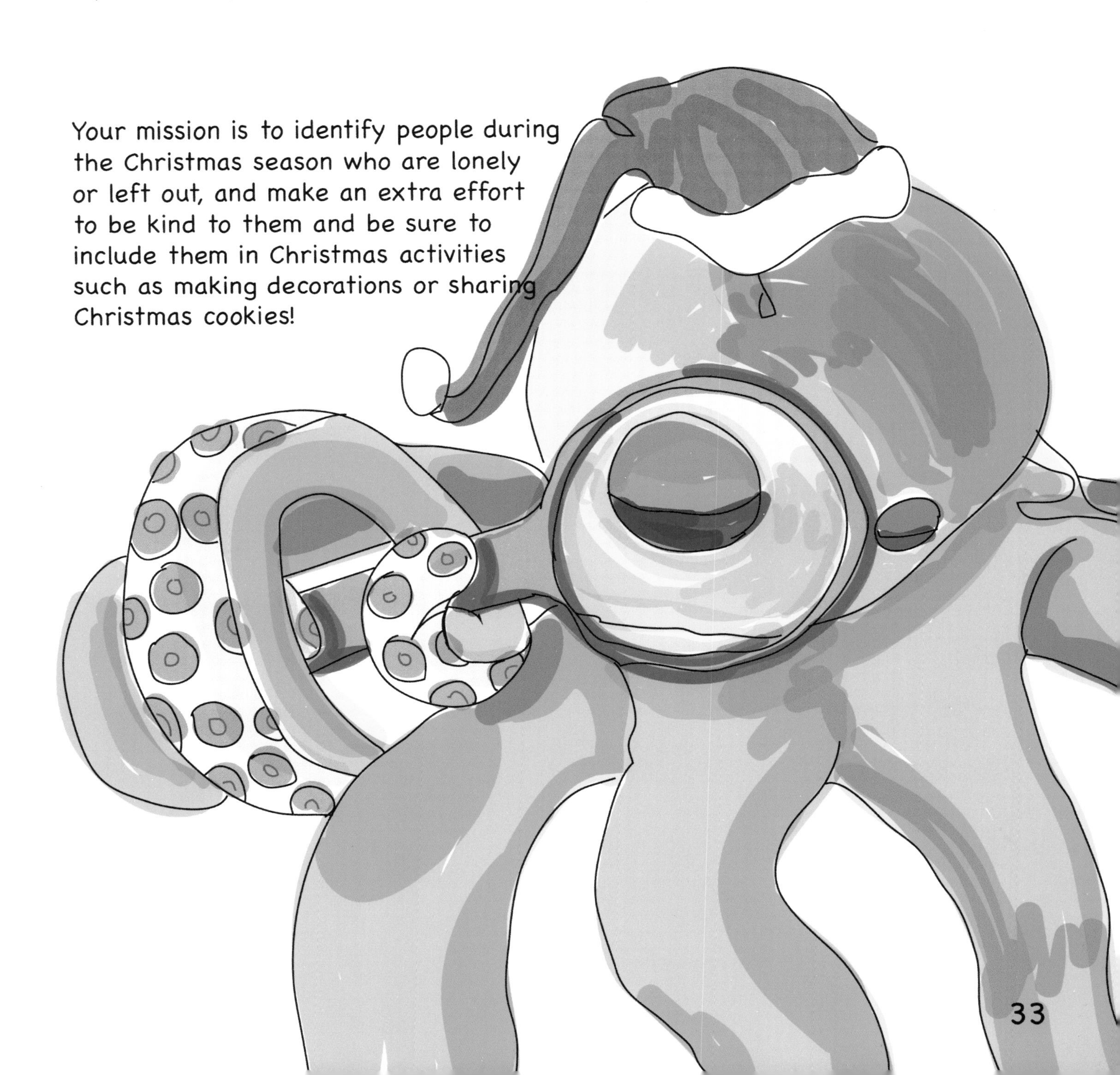

Elf enthusiasm

- Give everyone a big smile for no reason!
- Wish everyone you see a "Merry Christmas!" at school, in your neighborhood, at church, in the store, and everywhere you go.
- Hum or sing Christmas carols.
- Make Christmas decorations for your room and your home. We have included ideas for decorations in this book.

Decorating with shapes

Materials:

- Construction Paper
- Glue
- Scissors
- Options: Crayons/markers & assorted decorations, such as sequins, glitter, beads.

Decorating with shapes

Directions:

1. Trace the stocking pattern from page 38. Use the pattern to cut a stocking shape from construction paper.

2. Trace the cuff pattern at the top of the stocking. Use the pattern to cut a cuff for the top of the stocking from a piece of construction paper in a contrasting color.

3. Glue the cuff to the top of the stocking.

4. Trace the circle, square and triangle patterns from page. Use the patterns to cut a dozen of each shape from different colors of construction paper.

5. Glue the different shapes at random to cover the cuff and decorate the body of the stocking.

OPTIONS:

- Use crayons or markers to add designs to your stocking.
- Personalize - Write name on cuff and trim with glitter.
- Add some sparkle. Use sequins or beads to decorate cuff and stocking.

Decorating with shapes

Pattern from page 36

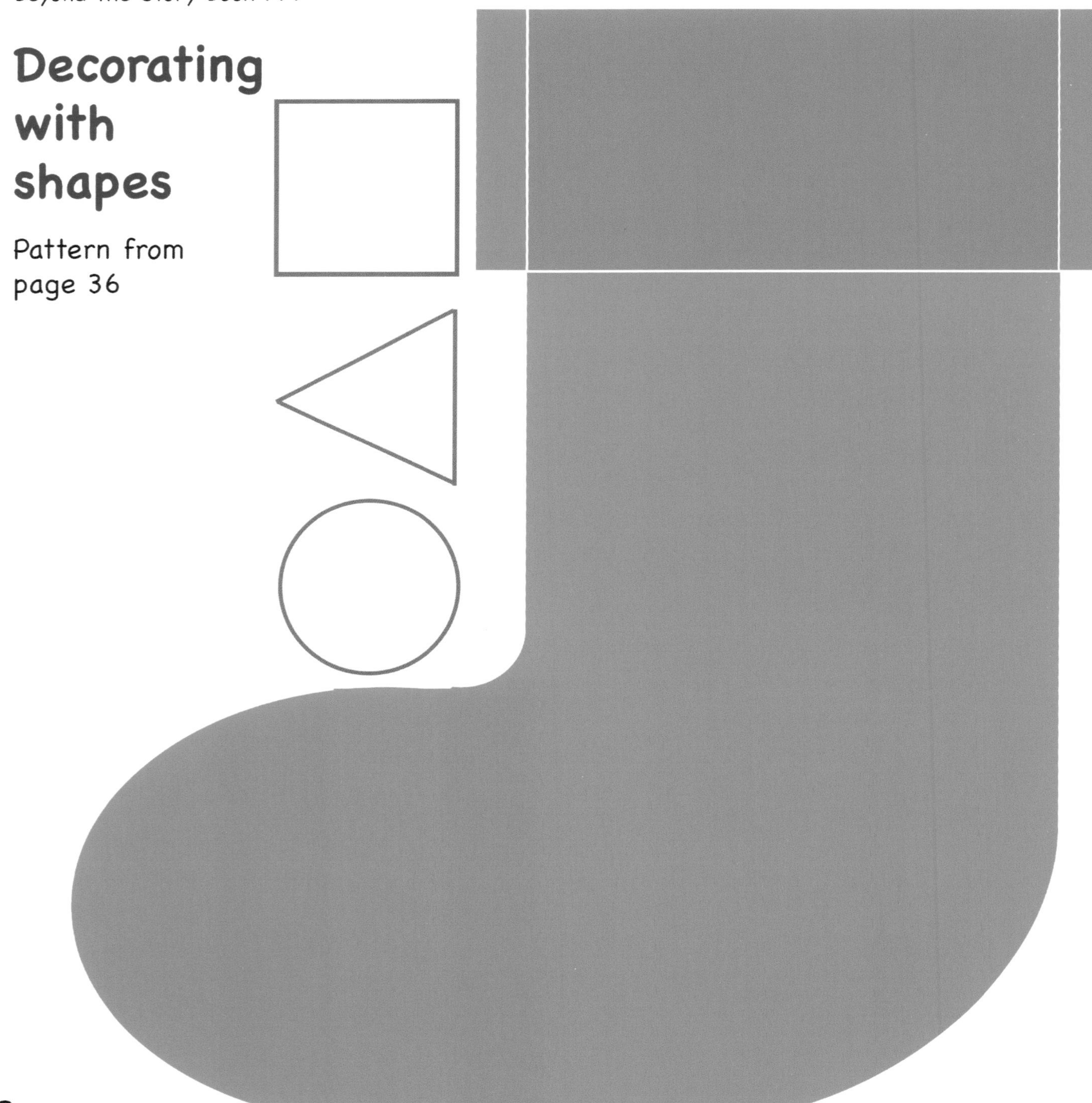

Shop for Santa:

Oh no! Santa's workshop is running behind. Santa needs your help to buy some gifts he still needs. He gives you $25.00 to buy more toys.

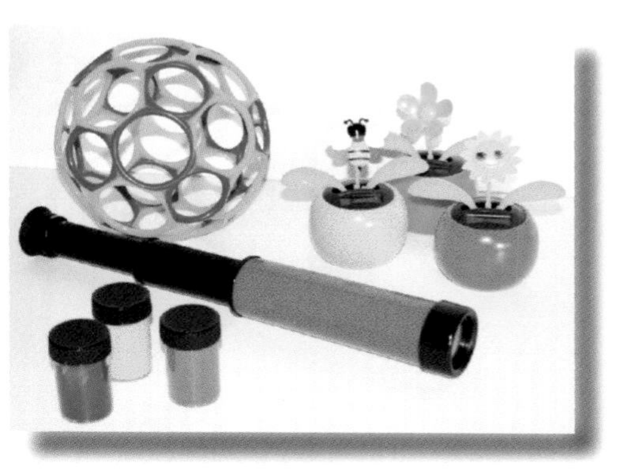

One **ball** is $ 5.00

One **paint set** is $ 7.00

One **flower pot set** is $ 8.00

One **telescope** is $12.50

1. Santa asks you to buy just the balls. How many balls can you buy? Will you have any change?

2. Santa must have one ball and one paint set, but asks you to also buy one telescope if there is enough money. Can you buy the ball, the paint set and the telescope? Will you have any change?

3. How many flower pot sets can you buy with Santa's money? Will you have any change?

4. Santa must have one telescope, and asks you to buy as many balls as you can with the rest of the money. How many balls can you buy? Will you have any change?

Find the answers on page 40

Shop for Santa answers

One **ball** is $ 5.00 - One **paint set** is $ 7.00

One **flower pot set** is $ 8.00 - One **telescope** is $12.50

1. Santa asks you to buy just balls, how many balls can you buy? Will you have any change?

   You can buy 5 balls.

   $5.00 + $5.00 + $5.00 + $5.00 + $5.00 = $25.00

   No change.

2. Santa must have one ball and one paint set, but asks you to also buy one telescope if there is enough money. Can you buy the ball, the paint set and the telescope? Will you have any change?

   Yes.

   $5.00 + $7.00 + $12.50 = $24.50

   Yes, $.50 in change.

3. How many flower pot sets can you buy with Santa's money? Will you have any change?

   You can buy 3 flower pot sets.

   $8.00 + $8.00 + $8.00 = $24.00

   Yes, $1.00 in change.

4. Santa must have one telescope, and asks you to buy as many balls as you can with the rest of the money. How many balls can you buy? Will you have any change?

   You can buy 2 balls along with the telescope.

   $12.50 + $5.00 + $5.00 = $22.50

   Yes, $2.50 in change.

Answers from page 39

Handprint wreath

Materials:

Construction paper
Pencil
Scissors
Glue
Paper Plate
Ribbon

Instructions:

1. Trace your handprint on different colors of construction paper and cut out. You will need 10 to 16 handprints to make the wreath.
2. Place the handprints in a circle before gluing. Using a paper plate as a guide, overlap your handprints in a circle.
3. Once you have the hands laid in the pattern, lift up each thumb, add glue to the bottom, and press back down to attach it to the piece of paper it overlaps. Work your way around the circle until all the handprints are glued together.

   Note: the plate is just to help create the circle. You do not need to glue the wreath to the plate.

4. Let the wreath dry.
5. Use ribbon to tie a bow and glue to the wreath for decoration.

"Gingerbread" Village

"Gingerbread" Village

Materials:

- Several decorated houses made from paper bags from the "Gingerbread" ornament instructions. (See page 44.)
- Craft sticks
- Styrofoam base, at least 1" thick, approximately 8" long and 3"wide.
- One piece of felt to cover bottom of the styrofoam base
- Cotton balls
- Glue

Instructions:

1. Make several houses with different decorations.

2. Glue a craft stick to the back of each house with 1" inch extending beyond the bottom edge of the house.

3. Cover the bottom of the base with felt, cut to the same shape and size, to prevent scratches.

4. Stick the houses into the foam base.

5. Glue cotton balls to the foam base around the houses for snow.

"Gingerbread" house ornament

Materials:

Brown paper bag
Scissors
Glue
Yarn or ribbon for hanger

Food items such as:

pretzels, mini-marshmallows, cereal pieces, raisins and gummy candy pieces.

Crayons, markers and construction paper for optional decorations

NOTE: Do NOT use hard sugar candies or candies with sugar shells. The glue will cause the sugars to dissolve, the colors will run and glue will not harden.

Instructions:

1. Trace the house pattern from page 45. Use the pattern to cut a house from the paper bag.

2. Use food items to decorate the house. Attach with glue and set aside to dry completely before adding hanger.

CAUTION! Do NOT eat any food items that have been glued. For decoration ONLY!

3. For the hanger, cut a 10" long piece of ribbon or yarn. Cut a 1" X 1" square from the paper bag.
4. Make a loop from the ribbon and gather the ends together. Glue the open ends of the loop to the back of the ornament. Glue the piece of paper over the top of the ribbon to help secure the hanger to the back of the ornament.

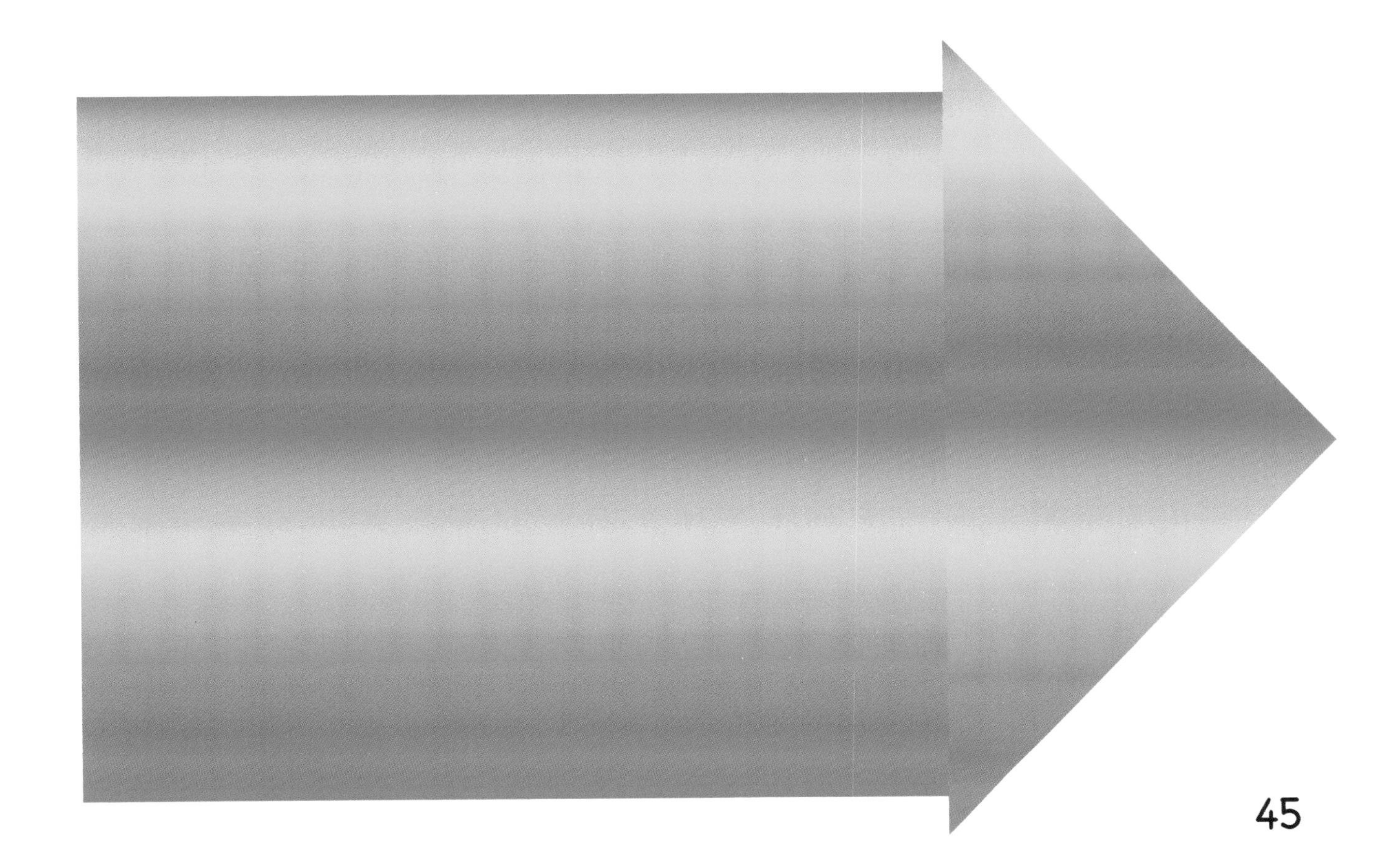

Other Baxter's Corner Books

Oakley the Octopus Series

**"For most of us, shaking hands is quite easy.
Shaking hands doesn't make us feel nervous or queasy."**

It is polite to shake hands when meeting new people. But which hand should an eight-handed octopus use? Oakley the Octopus is worried about being different. His teacher - Mr. Marvin McBoom - helps Oakley discover the benefits of his many arms, and Oakley comes to value his unique attributes.

Ellema the Elephant Series

**"Just imagine if your nose were as long as your arm.
Sneezing with that nose might create an alarm."**

With her long trunk, Ellema the Elephant causes quite a stir when she sneezes. When Ellema learns to control her sneezes, everything calms down. Perhaps things are too calm. Kite Day is nearly ruined when there is no wind ... until Ellema sneezes her biggest sneeze ever!

Fred the Frog Series

**"Jumping," thought Fred, "looks like wonderful fun.
I can't wait to grow legs and hop in the sun."**

As a tadpole, Fred can't wait to jump just like the older frogs. But one of Fred's new legs is shorter than the other, and the jumping coach tells Fred that maybe jumping is not for him. Instead of giving up, Fred figures out a special way to jump. He practices and practices ... until he can hit the target every time.

Ally the Alligator Series

**"No dad to coach soccer, to play games or read books.
No dad to ride bikes or take fish off of hooks."**

Tomorrow is Donuts with Dads Day at school. Ally the Alligator is not looking forward to this special event because she does not have a dad to invite. What will she tell everyone when she shows up alone? Everything turns around when Ally chooses to focus on what she has instead of what she is missing.

CPSIA information can be obtained at www.ICGtesting.com
Printed in the USA
LVIW01n1725191115
PP10249600001B/1